A NOTE TO PARENTS

Reading Aloud with Your Child

Research shows that reading books aloud is the single most valuable support parents can provide in helping children learn to read.

- Be a ham! The more enthusiasm you display, the more your child will enjoy the book.
- Run your finger underneath the words as you read to signal that the print carries the story.
- Leave time for examining the illustrations more closely; encourage your child to find things in the pictures.
- Invite your youngster to join in whenever there's a repeated phrase in the text.
- Link up events in the book with similar events in your child's life.
- If your child asks a question, stop and answer it. The book can be a means to learning more about your child's thoughts.

Listening to Your Child Read Aloud

The support of your attention and praise is absolutely crucial to your child's continuing efforts to learn to read.

- If your child is learning to read and asks for a word, give it immediately so that the meaning of the story is not interrupted. DO NOT ask your child to sound out the word.
- On the other hand, if your child initiates the act of sounding out, don't intervene.
- If your child is reading along and makes what is called a miscue, listen for the sense of the miscue. If the word "road" is substituted for the word "street," for instance, no meaning is lost. Don't stop the reading for a correction.
- If the miscue makes no sense (for example, "horse" for "house"), ask your child to reread the sentence because you're not sure you understand what's just been read.
- Above all else, enjoy your child's growing command of print and make sure you give lots of praise. *You are your child's first teacher — and the most important one. Praise from you is critical for further risk-taking and learning.*

— Priscilla Lynch
Ph.D., New York University
Educational Consultant

To Michelle, who still has lots of hop
— G.M.

To Samuel Gus Ziebel
and Jordan Emily Zwetchkenbaum
— B.L.

Text copyright © 1997 by Grace Maccarone.
Illustrations copyright © 1997 by Betsy Lewin.
All rights reserved. Published by Scholastic Inc.
HELLO READER!, CARTWHEEL BOOKS, and the CARTWHEEL BOOKS logo
are registered trademarks of Scholastic Inc.

Library of Congress Cataloging-in-Publication Data

Maccarone, Grace.
    Sharing time troubles / by Grace Maccarone; illustrated by Betsy Lewin.
      p.   cm. — (First-grade friends) (Hello reader! Level 1)
    Summary: Sam searches through all of his toys but can't find anything
good enough to take to school for show and tell until his troublesome little
brother appears.
    ISBN 0-590-73879-8
    [1. Sharing — Fiction. 2. Brothers — Fiction. 3. Schools — Fiction.
4. Stories in rhyme.]
    I. Lewin, Betsy, ill. II. Title. III. Series. IV. Series:
    Maccarone, Grace. First-grade friends.
PZ8.3.M217Sh   1997
[E] — dc20   95-36015
                                                CIP
                                                AC

12 11 10 9 8 7   9/9 0 1/0

Printed in the U.S.A.   23

First Scholastic printing, March 1997

Sharing Time Troubles

by Grace Maccarone
Illustrated by Betsy Lewin

Hello Reader! — Level 1

SCHOLASTIC INC.
New York Toronto London Auckland Sydney

It's Monday.
It is sharing time.

Dan brings his pet,
a frog named Slime.

It's Tuesday.
It is time to share.
Pam brings her special
Teddy bear.

On Wednesday, Max brings Mexican money.

Kim brings gold.

Jan brings
a bunny.

On Thursday,
Sam has nothing to share.
No pet. No gold.
No money. No bear.

At home, Sam looks
at all his stuff.
But none of it
is good enough.

Books, blocks, balls,
a baseball bat.
Cards and caps,
a cowboy hat.

Sam's little brother
wants to play.

But Sam has sharing time
troubles today.
Sam says, "Go away."

Then Sam says, "Stay!"

It's Friday, and Sam
has something to show.
"Can you guess what it is?"
Sam asks. "Do you know—

what's as sloppy as a frog,

as hoppy as a bunny,

as cute as a Teddy bear,
and better than gold or money?"

Jan makes a guess.
Dan makes another.
"I know!" says Kim.

"It's Sam's little brother!"